MW00958950

PRINCE MARTIN
AND THE THIEVES

PRINCE MARTIN

AND THE THIEVES

BOOK TWO OF THE PRINCE MARTIN EPIC

BY BRANDON HALE

Illustrated by
JASON ZIMDARS

To Mom, who let me play outside to my heart's content and showed me the true meaning of grit, and to Dad, who built me two wonderful treehouses and walked with me in the woods.
—B.H.

To my children, family, and friends—thank you for your kindness and for encouraging me to keep making art.
—J.Z.

CONTENTS

ACE SLASH TEAR

THE
BOSS

BOO

HOSS

CHAPTER 1

"Oh, what terrible luck! We have *got* to get free," Martin whispered to Ray as they hung from a tree.

"Never fear," said Sir Ray. "We'll get out of this mess." But the dog worried too—more than he would confess.

They were trapped by two snares of the peg-trigger kind. Just dangling there, they were sure in a bind!

They'd been flipped off their feet (hardly what they had planned), and the boy's trusty short sword had slipped from his hand. It now lay in the leaves, which had hidden the snares— that trapped our two friends as they walked unawares.

And to make matters worse, there were gathered beneath: five goons who were grinning *and armed to the teeth*! They'd emerged from the shadows, where they had all lurked. They'd been biding their time till our two friends were jerked right up off of their feet and then into the air. They had black leather jackets and dye in their hair. They all carried big clubs. They had knives at their hips. They had spikes through their noses, their ears, and their lips. They had shocking tattoos on their arms and their necks—that wriggled and writhed when these felons would flex. They had grizzled goatees. They looked ready to brawl.

Uh-oh! thought Ray, as he studied them all.

Ray had traveled the world. He had seen a whole lot. And he knew things that only experience taught. And he knew without doubt—he could tell by their looks—that these gangsters who'd got them were *specialized* crooks.

"We've been caught by the *brigands*," Ray whispered real low. "Don't reveal you're a prince—and they *might* let us go."

What are "brigands" you wonder? Well, let me explain! They're vicious and violent and greedy for gain. Through the ages, the world's known this criminal kind. They have preyed upon travelers for time out of mind. Known as "highwaymen," "road agents," "brigands," or "thieves," they prowl along coach roads with *tricks* up their sleeves. By deception—then force—they steal silver and gold. They're terribly daring, most brazen and bold.

This particular outfit was led by *The Boss*. One *bad* desperado you'd *not* want to cross! The Boss wielded a knife with a razor-sharp blade. And the glint in his eyes made men *very* afraid.

He was born in the south in the midst of a war. He grew up around bedlam and bloodshed and gore. As a boy, he'd been known by the name Robert Snooks. At fourteen, he ran off and fell in with some crooks.

He was twenty years old now—his mom's only son—oh, but *long* was the list of bad deeds he had done! Simply scan down a list of old common-law crimes: he'd committed each one of them *multiple times.*

There was one, in particular, Robert loved best. He had focused on it (though he still liked the rest). That offense was to rob people riding the roads—a serious crime in old criminal codes. He got hooked on the danger, the loot, and the thrills. He practiced a lot, and he polished his skills. He perfected his craft, which he raised to an art. He was cruel and daring and *wickedly smart.*

Robert formed his own gang, and they called him *The Boss.* Mounted high on swift horses, they traveled across dusty coach roads and highways; and driven by greed, his men always obeyed him. They followed his lead.

As the brains of the bunch, The Boss thought for them all. And while *they* were real big, he *himself* was quite small. Oh, but he was the meanest and scorned all the rules. He'd killed off his conscience for diamonds and jewels.

They would hide along coach roads, just lying in wait, and they'd stake out the coaches with high-value freight. By some trick of The

Boss's, the coach drivers slowed. They would roll to a stop—then his *true colors* showed! His five thieves would burst out with a big show of force. And *then* with no decency—zero remorse—he'd shout, "Stand and deliver! Your gold or your life!" If a coachman refused, they would widow his wife!

They had pillaged and plundered the plains in the south. And their bad reputation had spread word of mouth. These notorious outlaws, now known far and wide, had never been caught—though the law often tried.

They had ravaged the south—not much *there* left to steal. But The Boss wanted *more* in his criminal zeal. So he'd brought them out west on a quest for more bling. And they'd recently entered the realm of the King—the same realm where the Prince and the knight named Sir Ray were on foot in the forest that crisp autumn day.

And the thieves had been close, camping just off the road. They had hijacked a coach and made off with its load. Then they hid the two snares, not for gold, but *a meal*; they had set them for supper, not something to steal. They had worked up their appetites robbing the coach. It was *then* that they saw our friends blithely approach!

The gang captured them both. Now they hung from the oak. The thieves leered at our friends. And then one brigand spoke. He was brutish and big and said, "*What* have we *here?* I had hoped for *a wolf*—what with suppertime near. Oh, but *this* is much better—will *more* than suffice. (Though, I *do* like wolf stew, which would sure have been nice.)"

"We won't *eat* them, you dimwit! That won't do at all," said *The Boss* to the thief, in a thick southern drawl. He jumped down from the branch (where he'd hidden above), made his way to his prey with a push and a shove. The Boss studied his captives, then studied the ground. He kicked at the leaves, and among them he found . . . *Martin's crown!*

Then he grinned very wickedly *since* . . . he'd confirmed that the kid that he'd caught was *a prince!* (Yes, the crown had dropped too, right along with the blade, when they'd triggered those traps that these outlaws had laid.)

"This is our lucky day," said The Boss to his crew. "Mark my words, we'll be *richer* when *this* week is through: because dangling up there is the son of *a king*! Have you any idea the ransom he'll bring? We'll compose a quick note to this king that will say: 'If you want your kid back, then get ready to pay. Send a chest full of gold for your prince that we've got. And we'll throw in the mutt just to sweeten the pot.'"

His thieves nodded and grinned (they were *not* very bright). Then The Boss said, "It's settled. Who knows how to write?" Then they hemmed, and they hawed, and they studied their feet. They were pretty embarrassed, did not want to meet the pale eyes of The Boss who, though not very tall, had a *terrible temper* well known to them all.

He dramatically sighed.

To the Prince, he declared, "I've got *nothing* to work with here—*not* that you cared. I'll just do it myself. Maybe write it *in blood*"—and the glint in his eyes made the Prince's heart thud.

Then Ray growled at The Boss, who just started to laugh—then he viciously struck the bold dog with his staff!

The young Prince and Sir Ray, they were sure in a mess! Could they somehow escape? It was anyone's guess! Now you want to discover the fate of our friends.

But *beginnings* must come before jumping to ends.

CHAPTER 2

This adventure began just the morning before, when the King (Martin's father) assigned them a chore: "You must visit the Duke at his castle up north—an eighty-mile journey on foot, back and forth. It's his birthday tomorrow. I must send a gift. But my coaches are out, so you can't have a lift. You must travel on foot, sleep out under the stars. But enjoy the long walk through this kingdom of ours!

"It is forty miles there, and it's forty miles back. You should keep that in mind as you're starting to pack. Travel light. Travel fast. Only take what you need. Don't bring very much food, for the Duke's sure to feed you a meal when you get there; you'll get resupplied. Here's a map to consult; it will serve as your guide.

"As you make your way north, you must first make a stop—to pick up *the gift* at the metalcraft shop. You will pay for the gift with this pouch full of gold. What the blacksmith has made is fantastic, I'm told."

He entrusted the coins to his son and Sir Ray, and said, "Pack for your journey and set out today."

So they took what they needed then headed to town. People hailed their young Prince, with his sword and his crown.

Soon they walked through the door of the metalcraft shop, where the smith honed the edge of an ax with a strop. He was tanned from his forges of fiery heat. He had soot in his hair, on his clothes, on his feet.

Martin said, "We have come on behalf of the King," as he pulled out the pouch, and he loosened the string. It held sixteen gold coins, the agreed-upon price (not one more nor one less, for the King was precise).

And the blacksmith declared, "You must be

here for *this*!" as he gave the big ax an affectionate kiss. (He could also make horseshoes and wagon wheel spokes, which he perfectly fashioned with powerful strokes. But the blacksmith believed making *these* was a chore. What he *really* loved making were weapons of war!)

Martin paid for the ax with the pouch full of gold. And the weapon was *truly* a sight to behold! With a leather-wrapped grip and a head made of steel, the mere *sight* of this ax would make enemies reel!

"How's the sword?" the smith asked, as he eyed the boy's blade. "Did you know that's a sword my great-grandfather made?"

Martin drew out his sword, which the blacksmith admired. The man's ancestor's work had been truly inspired.

The boy sheathed the bright blade. The smith packaged the ax. He wrapped it up tight in some rough burlap sacks. It was worth a small fortune, so well was it made—surely worth every ounce of the gold the king paid. The smith promised the ax wouldn't falter or fail.

Then he showed them *another just like it for sale*!

Martin picked up the ax.

It felt *good* in his hands.

(Anybody who's held one himself understands. For there's nothing quite like the rich smell and the feel of a *battle ax* fashioned from leather and steel!)

But the boy had no gold of his own to disburse; he would stick with his short sword, for better or worse.

"But that ax's appeal is sure hard to ignore," Martin whispered to Ray as they walked out the door.

As the boy and the dog made their way through the town, they witnessed a scene that made both of them frown: walking out of the bakery, into the street was a tattered old tramp with no shoes on his feet. The tramp walked with a stoop—like he had a hurt back. It was clear that his life had got badly off track.

And the baker stepped out. He was dusted with flour, with his hands on his hips and his

face looking sour. He yelled, "Don't you come back here unless you can *pay!*" at the ragged old beggar, who hobbled away. The tramp went down the street with his head sadly bowed. And he soon disappeared; he was lost in the crowd.

The boy looked at the dog, and he felt quite confused. He just couldn't believe that the baker refused to give bread to the beggar—he *had* bread to spare!

And our friends had no food of their own they could share: for they still had a tiring journey ahead—and had *just enough* vittles to keep themselves fed.

And the baker did nothing to justify force: the choice and the bread were the baker's, of course.

And the boy had no money with which he could buy some fresh bread for the beggar, who'd just have to try to keep scrounging around in his search for a meal.

But it didn't seem right.

He continued to feel that he should have done *something* to ease the tramp's plight. But the beggar was gone now; he'd slipped out of sight.

Martin shook his head sadly and looked at Sir Ray. They had many more miles to travel that day. They continued their journey and stayed on the road that led forty miles to the Duke's grand abode.

CHAPTER 3

For a while, as they walked, that event seemed to loom in the travelers' minds, and it filled them with gloom.

But they hiked through a forest of towering trees, and the walk and the weather relieved their unease. For there's nothing quite like a long walk in the fall, with the leaves changing colors, the crisp air and all. *And to walk with a friend*! That's the *very* best way to travel about and keep sadness at bay.

Our two friends had first met barely three weeks before in a fight with some hogs—who were *bad to the core*. Ray had needed some help. Martin came to his aid. And *this* is the stuff of which friendships are made! The young Prince showed true grit when he conquered his fear. He and Ray fought the hogs, and they saved a young deer. They *decisively* won (not some stalemate or tie), but they suffered a lot—and Sir Ray lost an eye. Martin carried Ray home. It was *quite* an ordeal. But a friendship was forged that was stronger than steel!

Now they walked through the forest. Our friends traveled fast. They met no surprises, and through it, they passed.

And at dusk, the two travelers stopped for the night. After hiking all day, dinner *was* a delight! They had worked up their appetites; each cleaned his plate. They built a nice campfire and stayed up real late.

"Will you tell me a story?" the boy asked Sir Ray. "I love tales of adventure and lands far away!"

Ray had been a knight errant—brave, loyal, and true. He'd fought dragons and rescued a princess or two. So he told the boy stories of battles he'd fought, and strange places he'd been, and some villains he'd caught. But Sir Ray didn't boast. He was matter-of-fact. He didn't puff up—that's how *real* heroes act.

And he told of the night he'd spent locked up in jail—from a fight with some sailors who'd drunk too much ale. They had sailed into port after six months at sea. And they'd all gone ashore for a liberty spree. The crew hit all the inns and the taverns in town, and some sailors wound up at this place called The Crown.

And Sir Ray was there too.

He'd stepped in off the street—for a cool cup of milk, on account of the heat. Ray just minded his business. The sailors were plowed. They were very obnoxious, offensive, and loud. *Then one pinched a poor barmaid.* She felt so demeaned!

Ray saw it happen, so he intervened!

He went up to the sailor and said to his face, "Tell the lady you're sorry—then leave in disgrace."

When he wouldn't apologize, Ray cleaned his clock! His shipmates all stood there, jaws open in shock. They recovered their wits, though, and piled on Sir Ray. It was *five against one* in that fabulous fray!

Bottles broke on the floor—a whole ocean of booze, which mixed with the blood (which was mostly the crew's). Holes got knocked in the walls, where some punches had crashed. Many tankards and tables and barstools got smashed. And the place nearly *burned* when a lantern got broke! All the chaos grew worse, on account of the smoke.

The fight tore up the tavern. The constables came. The sailors skedaddled. But Ray took the blame.

As they led him to jail, though, the knight was in bliss: for that barmaid looked over and *blew him a kiss*!

Ray told *more* funny tales of tight spots he'd been in. The boy laughed, and he begged him to tell them again. And together they lay there out under the stars. They saw Leo and Lyra and Red Planet Mars. And they might have stayed up till the dawn's early light. But they needed some sleep, so they called it a night.

Our friends woke the next morning, bright-eyed and alert. (But the boy's back was sore after sleeping on dirt.) As they hiked to the castle, the home of the Duke, our friends had an encounter that *seemed* like a fluke.

From the woods off the road, they heard whines and a yelp. Was there someone in trouble? Perhaps they could help! The boy gripped his sword tight. The dog's ears were alert.

It sure *sounded* like someone was scared or was hurt!

CHAPTER 4

As they followed the sounds through the towering oaks, it occurred to them both that it *could* be a hoax.

"Maybe somebody's luring us off of the road," Martin whispered to Ray.

Their adrenaline flowed.

And the deeper they delved in that dimly lit wood, the more they both worried that somebody could jump right out and attack, catch them both by surprise! As they crept through the murk, our two friends strained their eyes. They were searching the forest for clues and for signs for they no longer heard all the yelps and the whines.

The whole forest grew quiet. The birds didn't

sing. The young Prince was on edge, coiled up like a spring.

It was *then* that they saw it: *a shadowy shape.*

For a moment they froze, and they stood there agape.

The dog's hackles shot up on the back of his coat. And a menacing growl rumbled deep in his throat.

Martin's hairs all stood up on the back of his neck. He felt plenty of fear, which he struggled to check!

When they took one step more, the shape *suddenly turned*! Two yellow eyes flashed! Like bright embers, they burned.

Martin knew, in an instant, despite the dim light, that the thing was *a wolf*—with a bone-crushing bite!

It had gleaming white fangs. It was lanky and lean. It snarled at them both. It looked scary and mean!

As it glared at our friends, though, they *boldly* glared back. The sides were both poised. Who'd be first to attack?

Martin bravely stepped forward and drew back his sword.

He started to strike—then he spotted the cord!

It was cinched to its foot, which was swollen and red! *Even if* it had wanted, it *couldn't* have fled.

Martin suddenly knew that the wolf was ensnared! He was hungry and thirsty—though fangs were still bared. He'd been caught by some scoundrel who wanted wolf stew or a warm winter coat or a mitten or two.

And despite the beast's growls, he was weakened and frail. Ray said, "*Let us help*. We can ease your travail."

The wolf stopped with the growling and slumped to the ground. He just stared at them both, and he made not a sound.

Martin freed the beast's leg with a swipe of his sword. He examined the cut, which the ground snare had scored. Then he gave him a drink and a hunk of jerked meat. Then he and Sir Ray helped him back to his feet.

The wolf said he'd been stuck there a couple

of days. Then he studied them both with a curious gaze. And he sniffed at their feet. He examined their tracks. (He was *wild,* of course; that's how *any* wolf acts.)

He said, "John is my name. I live deep in this wood." Then he told his new friends that the two of them could count on him to come help if they ever had need. He'd do all that he could to repay their good deed.

He would never forget.

He would pay them both back.

Then he bounded away to go locate his pack.

CHAPTER 5

For the boy and the dog, their long journey resumed. The castle loomed close. They arrived around noon.

They received a reception befitting a prince. The Duke served them lunch—and he spared no expense. And when Martin presented the ax to his host, he was clearly quite flattered and rose for a toast.

The Duke spoke of the King, and *profuse* was his praise. (Seemed he said the same thing in a few different ways.) And accustomed to speech of an old courtly style, the Duke talked, and he talked, for a *very* long while. When his flowery speech at last came to an end, Ray had fallen asleep sitting next to his friend.

The Prince jostled the knight, whispered, "We ought to leave. If we hurry, we'll make it halfway, I believe."

Ray awoke from his slumber. He stretched with a yawn. "That felt pretty good. But you're right: let's move on."

They gave thanks to the Duke for the sumptuous lunch. (He just *loved* his new ax, our two friends had a hunch!)

Then the Duke said, "Beware as you make your way back; you must be on your guard against sudden attack: for three days now, some thieves have been stalking our roads. They've been hijacking coaches and lightening loads. They attacked my own wagon! My driver got rolled! They took off with my chest that was brimming with gold!"

He explained he'd just harvested all of his grain. (It had been a good crop, on account of the rain.) He had hitched up his wagon and loaded his crop. Then his driver climbed up, and he sat there on top. The Duke bid him goodbye, and the driver set out. He took the King's highway, that well-traveled route. He arrived in the village and sold the Duke's grain. With a chest full of gold, he returned down the lane.

Driving back to the Duke's, down that dusty old road, something odd caught his eye—so the Duke's driver slowed. *What was that in the road?* The Duke's driver drew near. He got out of the wagon for it would appear that somebody lay hurt—and it *looked* like a boy. He ran to assist him. But it was a ploy! It was really a man, who was not hurt at all! He just *looked* like a boy: he was beardless and small.

The man wickedly grinned—then he pulled out a knife!

He said, "Stand and deliver! Your gold or your life!"

And then five other thieves appeared— bearded and big. And together these highway-men stole the Duke's rig! They got off with his gold. How would he pay his bills? His tastes were expensive, all ruffles and frills! And his driver had barely escaped with his life. The Duke said attacks just like this had been rife!

Thus, the Duke warned our friends with this frightening tale. After hearing this story, young Martin looked pale.

But he reached for his sword, which he'd recently won. (It had once been the King's, now belonged to his son.) "We'll keep watch for those brigands," the brave boy declared. "They're *not* going to find Ray and me unprepared!"

As our friends traveled home, they were feeling on edge. They imagined thieves lurking behind every hedge. But then after they'd spent the day walking in peace, their fears and their worries began to decrease.

The road led to the forest and took them inside, where the trees were quite dense—lots of places to hide. And they walked a long way in that dimly lit wood. They wanted to make it as far as they could.

Then they got to a spot where the trees were most dense. And Ray's hackles shot up, and he said to the Prince, "Something doesn't feel right. I don't like this a bit. The birds have gone silent; the squirrels have split."

When they took one step more, it was *then* the snares sprung! They flew up in the air, where they dangled and hung!

For the leaves had well hidden two snares from their view.

And behind the tall trees, there were *thieves* hidden too!

CHAPTER 6

They were shocked, and they frantically looked all around. The boy's sword and his crown lay below, on the ground.

Then five thieves sauntered out from the places they'd lurked. They looked up at the boy and the dog, and they smirked.

Leaping down from a limb, The Boss joined his five thieves—and discovered *the crown*, lying there in the leaves.

Now we've reached the same point where our story began. And I wish I could say that the pair had a plan. But our friends were quite caught—like two flies in a web. It was *here* that their fortunes had reached a low ebb.

Then The Boss wrote a note he addressed to

the King. And he greedily thought of the ransom they'd bring.

("And just how did this thief send that note?" you might ask. He assigned their poor pigeon this unpleasant task. And the note that the carrier pigeon conveyed told the King when and where they would meet for the trade.)

Then at nightfall, the thieves broke out bourbon and rum. They did not post a guard. They thought no one would come. Who would dare to confront them? Who'd dare interfere? What with all of their weapons, they'd nothing to fear. Then one pulled out a fiddle. They danced in the night. They were rowdy and rude, an embarrassing sight.

And they left our friends dangling, did not cut them down. "This is hard to believe," Martin said with a frown.

But Sir Ray was still cheerful, despite their tight spot. He said, "We'll never rest till these rascals are caught!"

Thus, the plight of our friends sure appeared pretty grim.

And that's when they heard a voice whisper to them!

"Would you care for some help?"

The voice came from the leaves! They did not move a muscle or hiccup or sneeze. They just stared into darkness in search of the voice. They'd take *anyone's* help; they did not have a choice.

Something moved a bit closer and crept through the leaves. Martin nervously looked down below at the thieves. But the brigands now slept. They all noisily snored, lying there with their weapons and ill-gotten hoard.

Then the light from the fire allowed them to see: something standing right there on the limb of the tree!

And that something they saw filled our friends with surprise: *a camouflaged elf,* with pale hair and gray eyes!

The elf spoke with a voice that was teasing— but kind—saying, "Somehow I'd never expected to find such unusual acorns adorning my oak!" (Martin wondered if this was some strange el-

ven joke.)

"I say 'my' oak," he whispered, "Of course, it's not *mine*." Our friends studied the elf, who seemed strange but benign. "I just tend this old forest," he whispered with pride. Then he pulled out a knife from the sheath at his side.

With a swipe of the blade, the elf cut our friends free. And they silently dropped to the ground from the tree. But the thieves slumbered on—they had partied too hard! (As I mentioned before, they did *not* post a guard.)

The elf hopped down beside them and said that they should slip away into darkness as fast as they could.

But Ray whispered, "Let's catch them, let's tie them up tight—put an end to their thievery, stop it tonight!"

"We're outnumbered," said Martin. "It's *six against three*. I say now that we're loose—since the elf cut us free—we should run to the village to summon the law." The bold dog agreed (though it stuck in his craw).

Then they turned to the elf, and they gave

him their thanks.

But *some* things make noises—loud clatters and clanks . . .

And when Martin crept over to where his things lay—which he wanted to grab before getting away—he bent down, and he gathered his crown and his sword.

It was *then* that they bumped—a most clangorous chord!

Martin stopped, and he froze!

What a *dreadful* mistake!

He looked at the thieves.

His knees started to shake.

CHAPTER 7

The thieves stirred.

And they woke.

And they jumped to their feet!

They all drew out their weapons, not missing a beat!

It was six against three—that is *not* a fair fight! And the Prince was to blame for their desperate plight.

"Don't you move," growled The Boss, "if you value your life!" He glared at the boy—and he pointed his knife. Though he weighed only ninety-eight pounds soaking wet, with his blade in his hands, The Boss posed a real threat!

With the elf at their side, our friends braced for a fight.

A deep voice then called out—and it split the dark night!

"Lay a hand on my friend, and I'll tear you apart."

The Boss was surprised, and he turned with a start! And then out from the shadows emerged a dark shape! The Boss couldn't believe it; he stood there agape.

The thing's *yellow eyes* flashed in the light of the fire!

Shining *fangs* were revealed for The Boss to admire! It was lanky and lean, and it glared at the thief.

And the boy was astonished—then sighed with relief: in the light of the fire, he recognized *John*! He had stealthily managed to sneak up upon the six thieves in the night. What a sight for sore eyes! Martin hadn't expected this pleasant surprise!

And then *eight other wolves* came, confronting the crooks, who were clearly concerned and exchanged nervous looks. For these wolves were not tame. They looked ready to fight. All those yellow eyes flashed in the bonfire light!

The five highwaymen looked for some sign from The Boss. This was quite unexpected. They felt at a loss.

And Sir Ray said, "It looks like the tables have turned!"

But The Boss had recovered. His *anger* now burned. And he lunged at the lad—quite a dastardly dare—as John the wolf leapt, and he flew through the air!

And the beast bit down hard on The Boss's right arm—half a second before that big blade could do harm! And the weight of the wolf dragged The Boss to the ground. They were evenly matched, inch for inch, pound for pound.

The foes rolled in the dirt. And their fight was a blur of glistening steel, gleaming fangs, and gray fur! The wolf dodged the thief's blade, which would slash at thin air! Then he'd fight with his fangs, which would rip and would tear. Oh, the sounds of their combat would curdle your blood: all the growls and snarls, the *terrible* flood of harsh curses that came from the mouth

of the thief. His minions were shocked, stared in pure disbelief!

Though their struggle was epic, it ended real fast! This was *not* John's first fight and would not be his last. When it came to a brawl, John was one of the best. Soon he stood there on top of his enemy's chest.

The wolf growled in his face and looked hard in his eyes. But the Boss looked away; he did *not* try to rise. He just raised up his hands—he'd run plumb out of fight. He *had* to surrender: he *feared* the wolf's bite!

When his gang saw him lying, immobile with fear, their own courage failed, and they didn't cohere. One thief bolted and ran, tried to get far away—but he wasn't as fast as the knight named Sir Ray! That bold dog ran him down, knocked him hard to the deck! Then he dragged the thief back by the scruff of his neck!

Another attempted to climb up a tree, an interesting choice: that was *one* way to flee. But the elf saw the thief, and his lasso soon whirled. He aimed at the bandit. His lasso unfurled. The elf *roped* the big rascal and jerked him right back! And the thief hit the ground with a bone-jarring smack.

There were three brigands left now; their chances were slim. Then Prince Martin stepped up and spoke sternly to them: "Drop your daggers and clubs and those swords to the dirt. If you quickly obey, no one *else* will get hurt!"

For a moment, the thieves thought they'd make a last stand. But they knew they were beaten, outmatched and outmanned. The young Prince looked so fierce with his crown and his sword—to say nothing of *wolves*, who could *not* be ignored! And that dog with those teeth! And that elf with his bow! Things were *much* different now than mere moments ago. So they raised up their hands. They admitted defeat. And they dropped all their weapons, which piled at their feet.

The elf tied the thieves up. They could not fight or run.

It was *then* the dawn broke: the first rays of the sun!

CHAPTER 8

Then the boy, dog, and elf thanked the timberwolf pack. John decided to stay, but the rest headed back.

As the wolves loped away to return to their lair, Ray looked hard at the thieves, and he said, "Don't you dare *even think* of escaping. *So far,* we've been nice. I'm warning you once. I will *not* tell you twice."

Then he said to his friends, "This is what we should do: we four-legged creatures can handle this crew. We'll have no trouble keeping these crooks under paw, while you two-legged fellows go summon the law."

"That sounds fine," said the boy, who then turned to the elf. Martin asked if he'd first tell them more of himself.

With a wink at the wolf, whom he'd met once before, the elf said that he hailed from a far distant shore. "I was born 'Theodosius,'" he sheepishly said. "But for obvious reasons, I just go by 'Ted.' I'm assigned to this forest. I tend to the trees. Taking care of this woodland is *my* expertise. I was deep in the woods when I got the report that some crooks had arrived of the very worst sort. A brave doe and her fawn brought this unwelcome news. I stopped where I stood. There was no time to lose. I made haste through the trees till I came to this site, where I saw the six thieves—and your terrible plight. I was glad I could help." The elf modestly grinned.

Then he said to the Prince, "We must hurry, my friend! Let's go climb to my treehouse, up high in my oak, where we'll send up some signals of puffy black smoke that will summon the Sheriff to ride here with speed—to lock these crooks up for their criminal greed!"

So the two of them left. Through the forest, they raced—to the treehouse where Ted's operations were based.

When they reached a huge oak, Ted announced, "Here's our stop. Now we climb, and we climb, till our ears start to pop."

The boy stood there in awe. What a sight to behold! The tree was *at least* several thousand years old! He could not see the top. Yes, the tree was that tall. Standing next to this wonder, he felt very small.

Then they started their climb. They moved up limb by limb. Martin followed the elf and stuck closely to him.

They, at last, reached a platform and stood there to rest. Martin panted for breath. His lungs burned in his chest.

"It gets easier now!" the elf said to his friend. Then he tugged on a rope.

They began to ascend!

For they stood on *a lift* Ted himself had devised.

"Hang on tight to the ropes," the elf gravely advised.

Then they glided straight up to Ted's home

in the sky: a towering treehouse, *five-hundred* feet high!

They stepped into the house through a red-painted door. (But they *first* wiped their feet on the mat on the floor!) Martin looked out a window and, my, what a view! Way up there, things looked different. The sky was so blue! There before him, he saw an expanse of great trees! And the clouds were so close, floating by on the breeze!

The elf went to his hearth, and he built a big fire, which belched out black smoke that went higher and higher. And the puffs of smoke signaled the crooks had been caught. Ted provided coordinates marking the spot.

Then he said, "While we wait for the Sheriff's reply, may I give you a tour of my home in the sky?"

The elf's house was a wonder—just what you'd expect of an elf who'd been told to preserve and protect a whole forest of trees and the creatures therein.

I'd like to describe it, but *where* to begin?

He had weapons aplenty affixed to the walls and coils of rope to prevent deadly falls. He had maps of the forest spread out for review. He had logbooks and charts and a portrait or two of the elves who had tended these trees long before. He had tall stacks of books full of Treetender lore. And to go with his lassos and arrows and bows, he had wardrobes that hung with his camouflage clothes.

Soon the Sheriff replied. They could see puffs of black; this ended the tour. Now the friends headed back.

They descended the oak, and they lit on the ground. They ran back to the place where the thieves had been bound.

CHAPTER 9

All the thieves were still there; they had not moved an inch. A *mere glance* from big John or Sir Ray made them flinch!

"A whole posse is coming," Ted said with a smile, "to lock up these thieves and commit them for trial!"

It sure didn't take long for the law to arrive. And the Sheriff was pleased they'd been taken alive. He had six different posters he slowly unrolled. Each depicted a man and said **WANTED!** in bold. He examined the thieves, who were inked up and scarred, then compared the six posters. He studied them hard. He looked back at The Boss, whom he loudly addressed: "Robert Snooks, you delinquent, you're under arrest!"

Then he said to the crooks who composed Robert's crew, "And I'm placing you cutthroats in custody too!"

Then among all the loot, Martin found a wood chest. And *it* was *the Duke's*, with his emblem and crest! It had been on his wagon—until it got robbed. When the chest was recovered, The Boss loudly sobbed!

Then the Sheriff announced he'd return all the loot. (He was honest and held in the highest repute.) Then he said the Duke posted a handsome reward for the person who captured the thieves and their hoard. He removed a small pouch, which he tossed to the boy. "Here are *sixteen gold coins*. They're now *yours* to enjoy!"

Then the posse connected the prisoners with chains, and they gathered up all of their ill-gotten gains. Then the Sheriff said, "Thanks," to the friends with a smile. And the lawmen set out with the thieves single file.

As they dragged him to jail, The Boss blubbered and cussed, as the rest of the gang looked away in disgust.

Now the four brave companions were all that remained. The boy couldn't believe all the gold he had gained! At first Martin was shocked, and he stood in a daze—then insisted they share it: "Let's split it four ways!"

But his friends wouldn't have it. They *all* three agreed that Prince Martin should keep it. They'd simply no need. It would just weigh them down. They had nothing to buy.

"I suppose that I'll keep it," he said with a sigh. The reward was now his to be spent as he wished. His three friends were so happy—two *tails* even swished.

Then Sir Ray said, "Why don't we head back into town, to that blacksmith, whose weapons have won him renown? Since it's market day, he'll be set up on the mall. He'll be hawking his steel from his weaponry stall."

And young Martin looked up, and he started to smile. He'd completely forgotten *the ax* for a while! (He'd been simply too busy to think of that ax—what with treehouses, bandits, and *timberwolf packs*!)

The companions thus walked till they reached the town square. And they got a few looks. People stopped just to stare. They went straight to the stall with the broadswords and mail. Martin hoped the great weapon would still be for sale.

And it was!

And the boy, he had *just enough gold*!

He must buy it up quickly—before it got sold!

The boy picked up the ax. What a sight to behold! With the ax in his hands, he felt daring and bold. He imagined himself going out for a ride, atop a great warhorse—*the ax* at his side . . .

Then a nearby commotion disrupted his thought—before the big ax had been wrapped up and bought.

They all turned to the scene, to the stall right next door.

Ray and Martin saw *someone* they'd *both* seen before: that bedraggled old tramp they'd seen begging for bread! He looked even worse. He still hadn't been fed. He had gone to the grocer's to beg for some food. But the grocer said, "Shoo!" He was snappish and rude.

The old beggar looked haggard and grizzled and gaunt. Martin looked at the ax, and he *badly* did want to complete the transaction—so strong was its grip.

This was quite a dilemma.

He chewed on his lip.

He looked back at the beggar, now sitting nearby. And he thought of the coins . . . and *what else* they could buy.

Then he turned to Sir Ray.

They exchanged a long look.

Then the Prince slowly put the ax back on its hook.

And he said to the blacksmith, "I think that I'll pass."

Then he walked towards the beggar, who sat on the grass. He went up to the tramp and said, "Pardon me, Sir."

The townspeople stared. He was causing a stir! Why on earth would *the Prince* go and talk to that man? He was tattered and filthy and smellier than some of yesterday's trash or a pig in his muck. Many eyebrows were raised. The tongues started to cluck.

The tramp *wasn't* the kind they preferred on their street; not a person to talk to or smile at or greet. He was not wearing shoes. He was missing some teeth. He'd just tramped into town and ranked way down beneath all the townsfolk, who viewed the poor man with disdain. Could he not just move on? Oh, why *must* he remain? He just wasn't the type that they wanted around. So when Martin approached him, they grimaced and frowned.

But the Prince didn't care.

No, Prince Martin *knelt low* by the beggar, who flinched as if fearing a blow. And the Prince touched his arm, looked him right in the eyes. The man timidly stared, full of shock and surprise. It had sure been awhile since he'd felt a kind touch—and he thought of a hound, whom he missed very much.

"What's your name?" asked the Prince.

"The name's Tim," he replied.

"Will you tell me your story?"

The poor fellow sighed.

The tramp spoke in a drawl, and he told of his past. He'd had a good life—but it unraveled fast. He was born in the south, and he'd fought in the war. Then he'd worked many years in a mapmaker's store. He had saved up his wages with one goal in mind: he would buy the first coach (that was cheap) he could find.

Tim at last bought a coach, and he'd ridden the roads, driving village to village delivering loads. He had only one friend: a dependable hound, who would sit there beside him as Tim rode around.

And then one day some brigands jumped out to attack!

Tim tried to resist—but the thieves *broke his back*. Then they kicked out some teeth. And they busted his head. They drove off in his coach—and they left him for dead. And the worst part of all was the fate of the hound, who lay quiet and still, beside Tim on the ground.

Tim had somehow survived—but could not earn a wage: he was three-quarters crippled and starting to age.

That was three long years past—and he'd begged ever since.

That was the story the tramp told the Prince.

The Prince paused for a moment, absorbing the tale. He was no longer thinking of axes for sale. Then he pulled out his pouch, which he put in the hand of the man, who just stared and did not understand.

The Prince smiled at the man, and he said, "It won't bite."

The man slowly untied it. And oh, what a sight! He just couldn't believe it. Was *this* a cruel joke? A small crowd had now gathered, but nobody spoke.

"With these sixteen gold coins, you won't hunger again," said the Prince to the man, with a shy, boyish grin. "It will pay for a room. No more nights on the street—it gets colder out

west: we get snowfall and sleet. And there might be enough to acquire a team of two mules and a coach to rekindle your dream."

Tim's eyes narrowed, at first, then they opened up wide. They filled up with tears. And the old fellow cried.

Then the Prince helped him up, got him back to his feet.

Tim smiled at the Prince.

And he said, *"Time to eat!"*

EPILOGUE

The Prince blushed just a bit as he walked to his friends. He had learned that kind acts always pay dividends: they had helped out the wolf, who then said he'd help them. Then the Treetender helped when they'd hung from the limb. Then the beast paid them back: yes, it sure saved the day when big John and his wolf pack had jumped in the fray! This had helped them recover the Duke's precious chest. How it all came together, well, who would have guessed?

And from that moment on, good Prince Martin would heed any person he found who was hurt or in need.

Thus, we end this old tale, but for this ep-

ilogue: the Prince and the elf and the wolf and the dog formed a brotherly band with the Prince at the helm. They had *many* adventures all over the realm. And they strove to do good. They tried hard to live right. They were ready and willing to fight the good fight.

Oh, but all was not well!

In a mountain back east, *two dragons woke up.*

And these drakes craved a feast . . .

THE END

FREE BONUS

Get FREE *Prince Martin and the Thieves* coloring book pages! You can print them from your home printer for immediate creative fun!

It's a FREE download at:
www.princemartin.com/coloringpages/

• • •

Don't miss *Prince Martin Wins His Sword*—Book One in the Prince Martin Epic—in which Martin meets Ray for the first time in an unforgettable adventure.
Find it at: *www.princemartin.com*

ABOUT THE AUTHOR

When Brandon Hale was a young boy, he lived in South America. It was a great place to be a kid, and his mom let him play outside as much as he wanted. He had a dog named Okie, a slingshot, and an awesome tree house his dad built. The tree was full of pink mangoes, jabbering parrots, and fat iguanas! When he was older, his family moved home to Oklahoma, and he began second grade. His favorite classes were Reading and History. He still got to spend a lot of time outdoors, and sometimes his uncles would take him hunting—with their falcons! His favorite tales were *Treasure Island*, *The Swiss Family Robinson*, *Old Yeller*, and *The Hobbit*.

After finishing 19 years(!) of school, Brandon went to work as an attorney. In 2001, a very beautiful lady agreed to marry Brandon. Now they have five great kids and live on the Oklahoma plains. Regarding Prince Martin, Brandon didn't even know he existed until he popped into his head one day! And when he had to go overseas for a long time in 2015, Brandon would tell his young son Prince Martin stories on the phone. In fact, the boy named some of the most important characters! Now Brandon wakes up real early every morning (when the house is unusually quiet) and writes about Prince Martin. *Prince Martin and the Thieves* is his second book—and he's got more up his sleeve!

ABOUT THE ILLUSTRATOR

Jason Zimdars is an artist and designer who has always loved to draw. He grew up immersed in stories of heroes and magic like *The Lord of the Rings*, *Star Wars*, *The Dark Crystal*, and *E.T.* He always came home from the movies or the library to draw all the amazing characters and places he saw in his imagination.

When his friend, Brandon, told him about Prince Martin he knew he had to draw him and all his friends, too. *Prince Martin and the Thieves* is his second book. He can't wait to share more of Prince Martin's adventures with you!

Mr. Zimdars lives in Oklahoma with his teenage daughter and two dogs, who aren't nearly as brave as Sir Ray.

For More Information

www.princemartin.com
info@princemartin.com

This is a work of fiction. Names, characters, places, and incidents either are the products of the author's imagination or are used fictitiously. Any resemblance to actual persons, living or dead, businesses, companies, events, or locales is entirely coincidental.

Copyright © 2017 Brandon Hale.
Illustrations Copyright © 2017 Jason Zimdars

All rights reserved. No part of this publication may be reproduced, distributed, or transmitted in any form or by any means, including photocopying, recording, or other electronic or mechanical methods, without the prior written permission of the author, except in the case of brief quotations embodied in critical reviews and certain other noncommercial uses permitted by copyright law.

Cover by Jason Zimdars.

Made in the USA
Monee, IL
14 January 2021

57604667R00057